The Case Of The Golden Bullet

by

Grace Isabel Colbron and Augusta Groner

Double9
BOOKS

The Case Of The Golden Bullet
by Grace Isabel Colbron and Augusta Groner

ISBN: 978-93-56569-31-7

Published by

DOUBLE 9 BOOKS

2/13-B, Ansari Road
Daryaganj, New Delhi – 110002
info@double9books.com
www.double9books.com
Tel. 011-40042856

This book is under public domain

Printed in India.

ABOUT THE AUTHOR

Austrian author Auguste Groner (née Kopallik; 16 April 1850 - 7 March 1929) is best known for her detective fiction. She also published works using the pseudonyms Olaf Björnson and A. the Metis, Renorga, and Paura.

The daughter of an accountant, Auguste Groner was born in Vienna, Austria, in 1850. Franz Kopallik, a painter, and Josef Kopallik, a theologian, were two of her brothers. She received her education in Vienna, at the Vienna Woman's Teacher Training Institute as well as the painting program at the Vienna Museum of Applied Arts. She served as a primary school teacher in Vienna from 1876 to 1905. She wed lexicographer and journalist Richard Groner in 1879. She started writing in the early 1880s, primarily historical and children's fiction.

She switched to writing crime fiction around 1890, creating Joseph Müller, the first serial police detective in German crime literature, who makes his debut in the 1890 novella The Case of the Pocket Diary Found in the Snow. She is best known outside of Austria for her crime fiction.

CONTENTS

INTRODUCTION
TO JOE MULLER

Joseph Muller, Secret Service detective of the Imperial Austrian police, is one of the great experts in his profession. In personality he differs greatly from other famous detectives. He has neither the impressive authority of Sherlock Holmes, nor the keen brilliancy of Monsieur Lecoq. Muller is a small, slight, plain-looking man, of indefinite age, and of much humbleness of mien. A naturally retiring, modest disposition, and two external causes are the reasons for Muller's humbleness of manner, which is his chief characteristic. One cause is the fact that in early youth a miscarriage of justice gave him several years in prison, an experience which cast a stigma on his name and which made it impossible for him, for many years after, to obtain honest employment. But the world is richer, and safer, by Muller's early misfortune. For it was this experience which threw him back on his own peculiar talents for a livelihood, and drove him into the police force. Had he been able to enter any other profession, his genius might have been stunted to a mere pastime, instead of being, as now, utilised for the public good.

Then, the red tape and bureaucratic etiquette which attaches to every governmental department, puts the secret service men of the Imperial police on a par with the lower ranks of the subordinates. Muller's official rank is scarcely much higher than that of a policeman, although kings and councillors consult him and the Police Department realises to the full what a treasure it has in him. But official red tape, and his early misfortune... prevent the giving of any higher official standing to even such a genius. Born and bred to such conditions,

Muller understands them, and his natural modesty of disposition asks for no outward honours, asks for nothing but an income sufficient for his simple needs, and for aid and opportunity to occupy himself in the way he most enjoys.

Joseph Muller's character is a strange mixture. The kindest-hearted man in the world, he is a human bloodhound when once the lure of the trail has caught him. He scarcely eats or sleeps when the chase is on, he does not seem to know human weakness nor fatigue, in spite of his frail body. Once put on a case his mind delves and delves until it finds a clue, then something awakes within him, a spirit akin to that which holds the bloodhound nose to trail, and he will accomplish the apparently impossible, he will track down his victim when the entire machinery of a great police department seems helpless to discover anything. The high chiefs and commissioners grant a condescending permission when Muller asks, "May I do this? ... or may I handle this case this way?" both parties knowing all the while that it is a farce, and that the department waits helpless until this humble little man saves its honour by solving some problem before which its intricate machinery has stood dazed and puzzled.

This call of the trail is something that is stronger than anything else in Muller's mentality, and now and then it brings him into conflict with the department,... or with his own better nature. Sometimes his unerring instinct discovers secrets in high places, secrets which the Police Department is bidden to hush up and leave untouched. Muller is then taken off the case, and left idle for a while if he persists in his opinion as to the true facts. And at other times, Muller's own warm heart gets him into trouble. He will track down his victim, driven by the power in his soul which is stronger than all volition; but when he has this victim in the net, he will sometimes discover him to be a much finer, better man than the other individual, whose wrong at this particular criminal's hand set in motion the machinery of justice. Several times that has happened to Muller, and each time his heart got the better of his professional instincts, of his practical common-sense, too, perhaps,... at least as far as his own advancement was concerned, and he warned the victim, defeating his own work. This peculiarity of Muller's character caused his undoing at last, his official undoing that is, and compelled his retirement from the force. But his advice is often sought unofficially by the Department, and to those who know, Muller's hand can be seen in the unravelling of many a famous case.

The following stories are but a few of the many interesting cases that have come within the experience of this great detective. But they give a fair portrayal of Muller's peculiar method of working, his looking on himself as merely an humble member of the Department, and the comedy of his acting under "official orders" when the Department is in reality following out his directions.

THE CASE OF
THE GOLDEN BULLET

"Please, sir, there is a man outside who asks to see you."

"What does he want?" asked Commissioner Horn, looking up.

"He says he has something to report, sir."

"Send him in, then."

The attendant disappeared, and the commissioner looked up at the clock. It was just striking eleven, but the fellow official who was to relieve him at that hour had not yet appeared. And if this should chance to be a new case, he would probably be obliged to take it himself. The commissioner was not in a very good humour as he sat back to receive the young man who entered the room in the wake of the attendant. The stranger was a sturdy youth, with an unintelligent, good-natured face. He twisted his soft hat in his hands in evident embarrassment, and his eyes wandered helplessly about the great bare room.

"Who are you?" demanded the commissioner.

"My name is Dummel, sir, Johann Dummel."

"And your occupation?"

"My occupation? Oh, yes, I—I am a valet, valet to Professor Fellner."

The commissioner sat up and looked interested. He knew Fellner personally and liked him. "What have you to report to me?" he asked eagerly.

"I—I don't know whether I ought to have come here, but at home—"

"Well, is anything the matter?" insisted Horn.

"Why, sir, I don't know; but the Professor—he is so still—he doesn't answer."

Horn sprang from his chair. "Is he ill?" he asked.

"I don't know, sir. His room is locked—he never locked it before."

"And you are certain he is at home?"

"Yes, sir. I saw him during the night—and the key is in the lock on the inside."

The commissioner had his hat in his hand when the colleague who was to relieve him appeared. "Good and cold out to-day!" was the latter's greeting. Horn answered with an ironical: "Then I suppose you'll be glad if I relieve you of this case. But I assure you I wouldn't do it if it wasn't Fellner. Good-bye. Oh, and one thing more. Please send a physician at once to Fellner's house, No. 7 Field Street."

Horn opened the door and passed on into the adjoining room, accompanied by Johann. The commissioner halted a moment as his eyes fell upon a little man who sat in the corner reading a newspaper. "Hello, Muller; you there? Suppose I take you with me? You aren't doing anything now, are you?"

"No, sir.

"Well, come with me, then. If this should turn out to be anything serious, we may need you."

The three men entered one of the cabs waiting outside the police station. As they rattled through the streets, Commissioner Horn continued his examination of the valet. "When did you see your master last?"

"About eleven o'clock last evening."

"Did you speak with him then?

"No, I looked through the keyhole."

"Oh, indeed; is that a habit of yours?"

Dummel blushed deeply, but his eyes flashed, and he looked angry.

"No, it is not, sir," he growled. "I only did it this time because I was anxious about the master. He's been so worked up and nervous the last few days. Last night I went to the theatre, as I always do Saturday evenings. When I returned, about half-past ten it was, I knocked at the door of his bedroom. He didn't answer, and I walked away softly, so as not to disturb him in case he'd gone to sleep already. The hall was dark, and as I went through it I saw a ray of light coming from the keyhole of the Professor's study. That surprised me, because he never worked as late as that before. I thought it over a moment, then I crept up and looked through the keyhole."

"And what did you see?"

"He sat at his desk, quite quiet. So I felt easy again, and went off to bed."

"Why didn't you go into the room?"

"I didn't dare, sir. The Professor never wanted to be disturbed when he was writing."

"Well, and this morning?"

"I got up at the usual time this morning, set the breakfast table, and then knocked at the Professor's bedroom door to waken him. He didn't answer, and I thought he might want to sleep, seeing as it was Sunday, and he was up late last night. So I waited until ten o'clock. Then I knocked again and tried the door, but it was locked. That made me uneasy, because he never locked his bedroom door before. I banged at the door and called out, but there wasn't a sound. Then I ran to the police station."

Horn was evidently as alarmed as was the young valet. But Muller's cheeks were flushed and a flash of secret joy, of pleasurable expectation, brightened his deep-set, grey eyes. He sat quite motionless, but every nerve in his body was alive and tingling. The humble-looking little man had become quite another and a decidedly interesting person. He laid his thin, nervous hand on the carriage door.

"We are not there yet," said the commissioner.

"No, but it's the third house from here," replied Muller.

"You know where everybody lives, don't you?" smiled Horn.

"Nearly everybody," answered Muller gently, as the cab stopped before an attractive little villa surrounded by its own garden, as were most of the houses in this quiet, aristocratic part of the town.

The house was two stories high, but the upper windows were closed and tightly curtained. This upper story was the apartment occupied by the owner of the house, who was now in Italy with his invalid wife. Otherwise the dainty little villa, built in the fashionable Nuremberg style, with heavy wooden doors and lozenged-paned windows, had no occupants except Professor Fellner and his servant. With its graceful outlines and well-planned garden, the dwelling had a most attractive appearance. Opposite it was the broad avenue known as the Promenade, and beyond this were open fields. To the right and to the left were similar villas in their gardens.

Dummel opened the door and the three men entered the house. The commissioner and the valet went in first, Muller following them more slowly. His sharp eyes glanced quickly over the coloured tiles of the flooring, over the white steps and the carpeted hallway beyond. Once he bent quickly and picked up something, then he walked on with his usual quiet manner, out of which every trace of excitement had now vanished.

The dull winter sun seemed only to make the gloom of the dark vestibule more visible. Johann turned up the light, and Horn, who had visited the Professor several times and knew the situation of the rooms, went at once to the heavy, carved and iron trimmed door of the study. He attempted to open the door, but it resisted all pressure. The heavy key was in the inner side of the big lock with its medieval iron ornamentation. But the key was turned so that the lower part of the lock was free, a round opening of unusual size. Horn made sure of this by holding a lighted match to the door.

"You are right," he said to the valet, "the door is locked from the inside. We'll have to go through the bedroom. Johann, bring me a chisel or a hatchet. Muller, you stay here and open the door when the doctor comes."

Muller nodded. Johann disappeared, returning in a few moments with a small hatchet, and followed the commissioner through the dining-room. It was an attractive apartment with its high wooden panelling and its dainty breakfast table. But a slight shiver ran through the commissioner's frame as he realised that some misfortune, some crime even might be waiting for them on the other side of the closed door. The bedroom door also was locked on the inside, and after some moments of knocking and calling, Horn set the hatchet to the framework just as the bell of the house-door pealed out.

With a cracking and tearing of wood the bedroom door fell open, and in the same moment Muller and the physician passed through the dining-room. Johann hurried into the bedroom to open the window-shutters, and the others gathered in the doorway. A single look showed each of the men that the bed was untouched, and they passed on through the room. The door from the bedroom to the study stood open. In the latter room the shutters were tightly closed, and the lamp had long since gone out. But sufficient light fell through the open bedroom door for the men to see the figure of the Professor seated at his desk, and when Johann had opened the shutters, it was plain to all that the silent figure before them was that of a corpse.

"Heart disease, probably," murmured the physician, as he touched the icy forehead. Then he felt the pulse of the stiffened hand from which the pen had fallen in the moment of death, raised the drooping head and lifted up the half-closed eyelids. The eyes were glazed.

The others looked on in silence. Horn was very pale, and his usually calm face showed great emotion. Johann seemed quite beside himself, the tears rolled down his cheeks unhindered. Muller stood without a sign of life, his sallow face seemed made of bronze; he was watching and listening. He seemed to hear and see what no one else could see or hear. He smiled slightly when the doctor spoke of "heart disease," and his eyes fell on the revolver that lay near the dead man's hand on the desk. Then he shook his head, and then he started suddenly. Horn noticed the movement; it was in the moment when the physician raised up the sunken figure that had fallen half over the desk.

"He was killed by a bullet," said Muller.

"Yes, that was it," replied the doctor. With the raising of the body the dead man's waistcoat fell back into its usual position, and they could see a little round hole in his shirt. The doctor opened the shirt bosom and pointed to a little wound in the Professor's left breast. There were scarcely three or four drops of blood visible. The hemorrhage had been internal.

"He must have died at once, without suffering," said the physician.

"He killed himself—he killed himself," murmured Johann, as if bewildered.

"It's strange that he should have found time to lay down the revolver before he died," remarked Horn. Johann put out his hand and raised the weapon before Horn could prevent him. "Leave that pistol where it was," commanded the commissioner. "We have to look into this matter more closely."

The doctor turned quickly. "You think it was a murder?" he exclaimed. "The doors were both locked on the inside—where could the murderer be?"

"I don't pretend to see him myself yet. But our rule is to leave things as they are discovered, until the official examination. Muller, did you shut the outer door?"

"Yes, sir; here is the key."

"Johann, are there any more keys for the outer door?"

"Yes, sir. One more, that is, for the third was lost some months ago. The Professor's own key ought to be in the drawer of the little table beside the bed."

"Will you please look for it, Muller?"

Muller went into the bedroom and soon returned with the key, which he handed to the commissioner. The detective had found something else in the little table drawer—a tortoise-shell hairpin, which he had carefully hidden in his own pocket before rejoining the others.

Horn turned to the servant again. "How many times have you been out of the apartment since last night?"

"Once only, sir, to go to the police station to fetch you."

"And you locked the door behind you?"

"Why, yes, sir. You saw that I had to turn the key twice to let you in."

Horn and Muller both looked the young man over very carefully. He seemed perfectly innocent, and their suspicion that he might have turned the key in pretense only, soon vanished. It would have been a foolish suspicion anyway. If he were in league with the murderer, he could have let the latter escape with much more safety during the night. Horn let his eyes wander about the rooms again, and said slowly: "Then the murderer is still here—or else—"

"Or else?" asked the doctor.

"Or else we have a strange riddle to solve."

Johann had laid the pistol down again. Muller stretched forth his hand and took it up. He looked at it a moment, then handed it to the commissioner. "We have to do with a murder here. There was not a shot fired from this revolver, for every chamber is still loaded. And there is no other weapon in sight," said the detective quietly.

"Yes, he was murdered. This revolver is fully loaded. Let us begin the search at once." Horn was more excited than he cared to show.

Johann looked about in alarm, but when he saw the others beginning to peer into every corner and every cupboard, he himself joined in the man-hunt. A quarter of an hour later, the four men relinquished their fruitless efforts and gathered beside the corpse again.

"Doctor, will you have the kindness to report to the head Commissioner of Police, and to order the taking away of the body? We will look about for some motive for this murder in the meantime," said Horn, as he held out his hand to the physician.

Muller walked out to the door of the house with the doctor.

"Do you think this valet did it?" asked the physician softly.

"He? Oh, dear, no," replied the detective scornfully.

"You think he's too stupid? But this stupidity might be feigned."

"It's real enough, doctor."

"But what do you think about it—you, who have the gift of seeing more than other people see, even if it does bring you into disfavour with the Powers that Be?"

"Then you don't believe me yet?"

"You mean about the beautiful Mrs. Kniepp?"

"And yet I tell you I am right. It was an intentional suicide."

"Muller, Muller, you must keep better watch over your imagination and your tongue! It is a dangerous thing to spread rumours about persons high in favor with the Arch-duke. But you had better tell me what you think about this affair," continued the doctor, pointing back towards the room they had just left.

"There's a woman in the case."

"Aha! you are romancing again. Well, they won't be so sensitive about this matter, but take care that you don't make a mistake again, my dear Muller. It would be likely to cost you your position, don't forget that."

The doctor left the house. Muller smiled bitterly as he closed the door behind him, and murmured to himself: "Indeed, I do not forget it, and that is why I shall take this matter into my own hands. But the Kniepp case is not closed yet, by any means."

When he returned to the study he saw Johann sitting quietly in a corner, shaking his head, as if trying to understand it all. Horn was bending over a sheet of writing paper which lay before the dead man. Fellner must have been busy at his desk when the bullet penetrated his heart. His hand in dying had let fall the pen, which had drawn a long black mark across the bottom of the sheet. One page of the paper was covered with a small, delicate handwriting.

Horn called up the detective, and together they read the following words:

"Dear Friend: —

"He challenged me—pistols—it means life or death. My enemy is very bitter. But I am not ready to die yet. And as I know that I would be the one to fall, I have refused the duel. That will help me little, for his revenge will know how to find me. I dare not be a moment without a weapon now—his threats on my refusal let me fear the worst. I have an uncanny presentiment of evil. I shall leave here to-morrow. With the excuse of having some pressing family affair to attend to, I have secured several days' leave. Of course I do not intend to return. I am hoping that you will come here and break up my establishment in my stead. I will tell you everything else when I see you. I am in a hurry now, for there is a good deal of packing to do. If anything should happen to me, you will know who it is who is responsible for my death. His name is—"

Here the letter came to an abrupt close.

Muller and Horn looked at each other in silence, then they turned their eyes again toward the dead man.

"He was a coward," said the detective coldly, and turned away. Horn repeated mechanically, "A coward!" and his eyes also looked down with a changed expression upon the handsome, soft-featured face, framed in curly blond hair, that lay so silent against the chair-back. Many women had loved this dead man, and many men had been fond of him, for they had believed him capable and manly.

The commissioner and Muller continued their researches in silence and with less interest than before. They found a heap of loose ashes in the bedroom stove. Letters and other trifles had been burned there.

Muller raked out the heap very carefully, but the writing on the few pieces of paper still left whole was quite illegible. There were several envelopes in the waste-basket, but all of them were dated several months back. There was nothing that could give the slightest clue.

The letter written by the murdered man was sufficient proof that his death had been an act of vengeance. But who was it who had carried out this secret, terrible deed? The victim had not been allowed the time to write down the name of his murderer.

Horn took the letter into his keeping. Then he left the room, followed by Muller and the valet, to look about the rest of the house as far as possible. This was not very far, for the second story was closed off by a tall iron grating.

"Is the house door locked during the daytime?" asked Horn of the servant.

"The front door is, but the side door into the garden is usually open."

"Has it ever happened that any one got into the house from this side door without your knowing it?"

"No, sir. The garden has a high wall around it. And there is extra protection on the side toward the Promenade."

"But there's a little gate there?"

"Yes, sir."

"Is that usually closed?"

"We never use the key for that, sir. It has a trick lock that you can't open unless you know how."

"You said you went to the theatre yesterday evening. Did your master give you permission to go?"

"Yes, sir. It's about a year now that he gave me money for a theatre ticket every Saturday evening. He was very kind."

"Did you come into the house last night by the front door, or through the garden?"

"Through the garden, sir. I walked down the Promenade from the theatre."

"And you didn't notice anything—you saw no traces of footsteps?"

"No, sir. I didn't notice anything unusual. We shut the side door, the garden door, every evening, also. It was closed yesterday and I found the key—we've only got one key to the garden door—in the same place where I was told to hide it when I went out in the evening."

"What place was that?"

"In one of the pails by the well."

"You say you were told to hide it there?"

"Yes, sir; the Professor told me. He'd go out in the evening sometimes, too, I suppose, and he wanted to be able to come in that way if necessary."

"And no one else knew where the key was hidden?"

"No one else, sir. It's nearly a year now that we've been alone in the house. Who else should know of it?"

"When you looked through the keyhole last night, are you sure that the Professor was still alive?"

"Why, yes, sir; of course I couldn't say so surely. I thought he was reading or writing, but oh, dear Lord! there he was this morning, nearly twelve hours later, in just the same position." Johann shivered at the thought that he might have seen his master sitting at his desk, already a corpse.

"He must have been dead when you came home. Don't you think the sound of that shot would have wakened you?"

"Yes, sir, I think likely, sir," murmured Johann. "But if the murderer could get into the house, how could he get into the apartment?"

"There must have been a third key of which you knew nothing," answered Horn, turning to Muller again. "It's stranger still how Fellner could have been shot, for the window-shutters were fastened and quite uninjured, and both doors were locked on the inside."

As he said these words, Horn looked sharply at his subordinate; but Muller's calm face did not give the slightest clue to his thoughts. The experienced police commissioner was pleased and yet slightly angered at this behaviour on the part of the detective. He knew that it was quite possible that Muller had already formed a clear opinion about the case, and that he was merely keeping it to himself. And yet he was glad to see that the little detective had apparently learned a lesson from his recent mistake concerning the death of Mrs. Kniepp—

that he had somewhat lost confidence in his hitherto unerring instinct, and did not care to express any opinion until he had studied the matter a little closer. The commissioner was just a little bit vain, and just a little bit jealous of this humble detective's fame.

Muller shrugged his shoulders at the remark of his superior, and the two men stood silent, thinking over the case, as the Chief of Police appeared, accompanied by the doctor, a clerk, and two hospital attendants. The chief commissioner received the report of what had been discovered, while the corpse was laid on a bier to be taken to the hospital.

Muller handed the commissioner his hat and cane and helped him into his overcoat. Horn noticed that the detective himself was making no preparations to go out. "Aren't you coming with us?" he asked, astonished.

"I hope the gentlemen will allow me to remain here for a little while," answered Muller modestly.

"But you know that we will have to close the apartment officially," said Horn, his voice sharpening in his surprise and displeasure.

"I do not need to be in these rooms any longer."

"Don't let them disturb you, my dear Muller; we will allow your keenness all possible leeway here." The Head of Police spoke with calm politeness, but Muller started and shivered. The emphasis on the "here" showed him that even the head of the department had been incensed at his suggestion that the beautiful Mrs. Kniepp had died of her own free will. It had been his assertion of this which, coming to the ears of the bereaved husband, had enraged and embittered him, and had turned the power of his influence with the high authorities against the detective. Muller knew how greatly he had fallen from favour in the Police Department, and the words of his respected superior showed him that he was still in disgrace.

But the strange, quiet smile was still on his lips as, with his usual humble deference, he accompanied the others to the sidewalk. Before the commissioners left the house, the Chief commanded Johann to answer carefully any questions Muller might put to him.

"He'll find something, you may be sure," said Horn, as they drove off in the cab.

"Let him that's his business. He is officially bound to see more than the rest of us," smiled the older official good-naturedly. "But in spite of it, he'll never get any further than the vestibule; he'll be making bows to us to the end of his days."

"You think so? I've wondered at the man. I know his fame in the capital, indeed, in police circles all over Austria and Germany. It seems hard on him to be transferred to this small town, now that he is growing old. I've wondered why he hasn't done more for himself, with his gifts."

"He never will," replied the Chief. "He may win more fame—he may still go on winning triumphs, but he will go on in a circle; he'll never forge ahead as his capabilities deserve. Muller's peculiarity is that his genius—for the man has undeniable genius—will always make concessions to his heart just at the moment when he is about to do something great—and his triumph is lost."

Horn looked up at his superior, whom, in spite of his good nature, he knew to be a sharp, keen, capable police official. "I forgot you have known Muller longer than the rest of us," he said. "What was that you said about his heart?"

"I said that it is one of those inconvenient hearts that will always make itself noticeable at the wrong time. Muller's heart has played several tricks on the police department, which has, at other times, profited so well by his genius. He is a strange mixture. While he is on the trail of the criminal he is like the bloodhound. He does not seem to know fatigue nor hunger; his whole being is absorbed by the excitement of the chase. He has done many a brilliant service to the cause of justice, he has discovered the guilt, or the innocence, of many in cases where the official department was as blind as Justice is proverbially supposed to be. Joseph Muller has become the idol of all who are engaged in this weary business of hunting down wrong and punishing crime. He is without a peer in his profession. But he has also become the idol of some of the criminals. For if he discovers (as sometimes happens) that the criminal is a good sort after all, he is just as likely to warn his prey, once he has all proofs of the guilt and a conviction is certain. Possibly this is his way of taking the sting from his irresistible impulse to ferret out hidden mysteries. But it is rather inconvenient, and he has hurt himself by it—hurt himself badly. They were tired of his peculiarities at the capital, and wanted to make his years an excuse to discharge him. I happened to get wind of it, and it was my weakness for him that saved him."

"Yes, you brought him here when they transferred you to this town, I remember now."

"I'm afraid it wasn't such a good thing for him, after all. Nothing ever happens here, and a gift like Muller's needs occupation to keep it fresh. I'm afraid his talents will dull and wither here. The man has grown perceptibly older in this inaction. His mind is like a high-bred horse that needs exercise to keep it in good condition."

"He hasn't grown rich at his work, either," said Horn.

"No, there's not much chance for a police detective to get rich. I've often wondered why Muller never had the energy to set up in business for himself. He might have won fame and fortune as a private detective. But he's gone on plodding along as a police subordinate, and letting the department get all the credit for his most brilliant achievements. It's a sort of incorrigible humbleness of nature—and then, you know, he had the misfortune to be unjustly sentenced to a term in prison in his early youth."

"No, I did not know that."

"The stigma stuck to his name, and finally drove him to take up this work. I don't think Muller realised, when he began, just how greatly he is gifted. I don't know that he really knows now. He seems to do it because he likes it—he's a queer sort of man."

While the commissioners drove through the streets to the police station the man of whom they were speaking sat in Johann's little room in close consultation with the valet.

"How long is it since the Professor began to give you money to go to the theatre on Saturday evenings?"

"The first time it happened was on my name day."

"What's the rest of your name? There are so many Johanns on the calendar."

"I am Johann Nepomuk."

Muller took a little calendar from his pocket and turned its pages. "It was May sixteenth," volunteered the valet.

"Quite right. May sixteenth was a Saturday. And since then you have gone to the theatre every Saturday evening?"

"Yes, sir."

"When did the owner of the house go away?"

"Last April. His wife was ill and he had to take her away. They went to Italy."

"And you two have been alone in the house since April?"

"Yes, sir, we two."

"Was there no janitor?"

"No, sir. The garden was taken care of by a man who came in for the day."

"And you had no dog? I haven't seen any around the place."

"No, sir; the Professor did not like animals. But he must have been thinking about buying a dog, because I found a new dog-whip in his room one day."

"Somebody might have left it there. One usually buys the dog first and then the whip."

"Yes, sir. But there wasn't anybody here to forget it. The Professor did not receive any visits at that time."

"Why are you so sure of that?"

"Because it was the middle of summer, and everybody was away."

"Oh, then, we won't bother about the whip. Can you tell me of any ladies with whom the Professor was acquainted?"

"Ladies? I don't know of any. Of course, the Professor was invited out a good deal, and most of the other gentlemen from the college were married."

"Did he ever receive letters from ladies?" continued Muller.

Johann thought the matter over, then confessed that he knew very little about writing and couldn't read handwriting very well anyway. But he remembered to have seen a letter now and then, a little letter with a fine and delicate handwriting.

"Have you any of these envelopes?" asked Muller. But Johann told him that in spite of his usual carelessness in such matters, Professor Fellner never allowed these letters to lie about his room.

Finally the detective came out with the question to which he had been leading up. "Did your master ever receive visits from ladies?"

Johann looked extremely stupid at this moment. His lack of intelligence and a certain crude sensitiveness in his nature made him take umbrage at what appeared to him a very unnecessary question. He answered it with a shake of the head only. Muller smiled at the young man's ill-concealed indignation and paid no attention to it.

"Your master has been here for about a year. Where was he before that?"

"In the capital."

"You were in his service then?"

"I have been with him for three years."

"Did he know any ladies in his former home?"

"There was one—I think he was engaged to her."

"Why didn't he marry her?"

"I don't know."

"What was her name?"

"Marie. That's all I know about it."

"Was she beautiful?"

"I never saw her. The only way I knew about her was when the Professor's friends spoke of her."

"Did he have many friends?"

"There were ever so many gentlemen whom he called his friends."

"Take me into the garden now."

"Yes, sir." Muller took his hat and coat and followed the valet into the garden. It was of considerable size, carefully and attractively planned, and pleasing even now when the bare twigs bent under their load of snow.

"Now think carefully, Johann. We had a full moon last night. Don't you remember seeing any footsteps in the garden, leading away from the house?" asked Muller, as they stood on the snow-covered paths.

Johann thought it over carefully, then said decidedly, "No. At least I don't remember anything of the kind. There was a strong wind yesterday anyway, and the snow drifts easily out here. No tracks could remain clear for long."

The men walked down the straight path which led to the little gate in the high wall. This gate had a secret lock, which, however, was neither hard to find nor hard to open. Muller managed it with ease, and looked out through the gate on the street beyond. The broad promenade, deserted now in its winter snowiness, led away in one direction to the heart of the city. In the other it ended in the main county high-road. This was a broad, well-made turnpike, with footpath and rows of trees. A half-hour's walk along it would bring one to the little village clustering about the Archduke's favourite hunting castle. There was a little railway station near the castle, but it was used only by suburban trains or for the royal private car.

Muller did not intend to burden his brain with unnecessary facts, so with his usual thoroughness he left the further investigation of what lay beyond the gate, until he had searched the garden thoroughly. But even for his sharp eyes there was no trace to be found that would tell of the night visit of the murderer.

"In which of the pails did you put the key to the side door?" he asked.

"In the first pail on the right hand side. But be careful, sir; there's a nail sticking out of the post there. The wind tore off a piece of wood yesterday."

The warning came too late. Muller's sleeve tore apart with a sharp sound just as Johann spoke, for the detective had already plunged his hand into the pail. The bottom of the bucket was easy to reach, as this one hung much lower than the others. Looking regretfully at the rent in his coat, Muller asked for needle and thread that he might repair it sufficiently to get home.

"Oh, don't bother about sewing it; I'll lend you one of mine," exclaimed Johann. "I'll carry this one home for you, for I'm not going to stay here alone—I'd be afraid. I'm going to a friend's house. You can find me there any time you need me. You'd better take the key of the apartment and give it to the police."

The detective had no particular fondness for the task of sewing, and he was glad to accept the valet's friendly offering. He was rather astonished at the evident costliness of the garment the young man handed him, and when he spoke of it, the valet could not say enough in praise of the kindness of his late master. He pulled out several other articles of clothing, which, like the overcoat, had been given to him by Fellner. Then he packed up a few necessities and announced himself as ready to start. He insisted on carrying the torn coat, and Muller permitted it after some protest. They carefully closed the apartment and the house, and walked toward the centre of the city to the police station, where Muller lived.

As they crossed the square, it suddenly occurred to Johann that he had no tobacco. He was a great smoker, and as he had many days of enforced idleness ahead of him, he ran into a tobacco shop to purchase a sufficiency of this necessity of life.

Muller waited outside, and his attention was attracted by a large grey Ulmer hound which was evidently waiting for some one within the shop. The dog came up to him in a most friendly manner, allowed him to pat its head, rubbed up against him with every sign of pleasure, and would not leave him even when he turned to go after Johann came out of the shop. Still accompanied by the dog, the two men walked on quite a distance, when a sharp whistle was heard behind them, and the dog became uneasy. He would not leave them, however, until a powerful voice called "Tristan!" several times. Muller turned and saw that Tristan's master was a tall, stately man wearing a handsome fur overcoat.

It was impossible to recognise his face at this distance, for the snowflakes were whirling thickly in the air. But Muller was not particularly anxious to recognise the stranger, as he had his head full of more important thoughts.

When Johann had given his new address and remarked that he would call for his coat soon, the men parted, and Muller returned to the police station.

The next day the principal newspaper of the town printed the following notice:

THE GOLDEN BULLET

It is but a few days since we announced to our readers the sad news of the death of a beautiful woman, whose leap from her window, while suffering from the agonies of fever, destroyed the happiness of an unusually harmonious marriage. And now we are compelled to print the news of another equally sad as well

as mysterious occurrence. This time, Fate has demanded the
sacrifice of the life of a capable and promising young man.
Professor Paul Fellner, a member of the faculty of our college,
was found dead at his desk yesterday morning. It was thought at
first that it was a case of suicide, for doors and windows were
carefully closed from within and those who discovered the corpse
were obliged to break open one of the doors to get to it. And
a revolver was found lying close at hand, upon the desk. But
this revolver was loaded in every chamber and there was no other
weapon to be seen in the room. There was a bullet wound in the
left breast of the corpse, and the bullet had penetrated the
heart. Death must have been instantaneous.
The most mysterious thing about this strange affair was
discovered during the autopsy. It is incredible, but it is
absolutely true, as it is vouched for under oath by the
authorities who were present, that the bullet which was found
in the heart of the dead man was made of solid gold. And yet,
strange as is this circumstance, it is still more a riddle how
the murderer could have escaped from the room where he had shot
down his victim, for the keys in both doors were in the locks
from the inside. We have evidently to do here with a criminal
of very unusual cleverness and it is therefore not surprising
that there has been no clue discovered thus far. The only
thing that is known is that this murder was an act of revenge.

The entire city was in excitement over the mystery, even the police station was shaken out of its usual business-like indifference. There was no other topic of conversation in any of the rooms but the mystery of the golden bullet and the doors closed from the inside. The attendants and the policeman gathered whispering in the corners, and strangers who came in on their own business forgot it in their excitement over this new and fascinating mystery.

That afternoon Muller passed through Horn's office with a bundle of papers, on his way to the inner office occupied by his patron, Chief of Police Bauer. Horn, who had avoided Muller since yesterday although he was conscious of a freshened interest in the man, raised his head and watched the little detective as he walked across the room with his usual quiet tread. The commissioner saw nothing but the usual humble business-like manner to which he was accustomed—then suddenly something happened that came to him like a distinct shock. Muller stopped in his walk so suddenly that one foot was poised in the air. His bowed head was thrown back, his face flushed to his forehead, and the papers trembled in his hands. He ran the fingers of his unoccupied hand through his hair and murmured audibly, "That dog! that dog!" It was evident that some thought had struck him with such insistence as to render him oblivious of his surroundings. Then he finally realised where he was, and walked on quickly to Bauer's room, his face still flushed, his hands trembling. When he came out from the office again, he was his usual quiet, humble self.

But the commissioner, with his now greater knowledge of the little man's gifts and past, could not forget the incident. During the afternoon he found himself repeating mechanically, "That dog—that dog." But the words meant nothing to him, hard as he might try to find the connection.

When the commissioner left for his home late that afternoon, Muller re-entered the office to lay some papers on the desk. His duties over, he was about to turn out the gas, when his eye fell on the blotter on Horn's desk. He looked at it more closely, then burst into a loud laugh. The same two words were scribbled again and again over the white surface, but it was not the name of any fair maiden, or even the title of a love poem; it was only the words, "That dog—"

Several days had passed since the discovery of the murder. Fellner had been buried and his possessions taken into custody by the authorities until his heirs should appear. The dead man's papers and affairs were in excellent condition and the arranging of the inheritance had been quickly done. Until the heirs should take possession, the apartment was sealed by the police. There was nothing else to do in the matter, and the commission appointed to make researches had discovered nothing of value. The murderer might easily feel that he was absolutely safe by this time.

The day after the publication of the article we have quoted, Muller appeared in Bauer's office and asked for a few days' leave.

"In the Fellner case?" asked the Chief with his usual calm, and Muller replied in the affirmative.

Two days later he returned, bringing with him nothing but a single little notice.

"Marie Dorn, now Mrs. Kniepp," was one line in his notebook, and beside it some dates. The latter showed that Marie Dorn had for two years past been the wife of the Archducal Forest-Councillor, Leo Kniepp.

And for one year now Professor Paul Fellner had been in the town, after having applied for his transference from the university in the capital to this place, which was scarce half an hour's walk distant from the home of the beautiful young woman who had been the love of his youth.

And Fellner had made his home in the quietest quarter of the city, in that quarter which was nearest the Archducal hunting castle. He had lived very quietly, had not cultivated the acquaintance of the ladies of the town, but was a great walker and bicycle rider; and every Saturday evening since he had been alone in the house, he had sent his servant to the theatre. And it was on Saturday evenings that Forest-Councillor Kniepp went to his Bowling Club at the other end of the city, and did not return until the last train at midnight.

And during these evening hours Fellner's apartment was a convenient place for pleasant meetings; and nothing prevented the Professor from accompanying his beautiful friend home through the quiet Promenade, along the turnpike to the hunting castle. And Johann had once found a dog-whip in his master's room-and Councillor Leo Kniepp, head of the Forestry Department, was the possessor of a beautiful Ulmer hound which took an active interest in people who wore clothes belonging to Fellner.

Furthermore, in the little drawer of the bedside table in the murdered man's room, there had been found a tortoise-shell hairpin; and in the corner of the vestibule of his house, a little mother-of-pearl glove button, of the kind much in fashion that winter, because of a desire on the part of the ladies of the town to help the home industry of the neighbourhood. Mrs. Marie Kniepp was one of the fashionable women of the town, and several days before the Professor was murdered, this woman had thrown herself from the second-story window of her home, and her husband, whose passionate eccentric nature was well known, had been a changed man from that hour.

It was his deep grief at the loss of his beloved wife that had turned his hair grey and had drawn lines of terrible sorrow in his face—said gossip. But Muller, who did not know Kniepp personally although he had been taking a great interest in his affairs for the last few days, had his own ideas on the subject, and he decided to make the acquaintance of the Forest Councillor as soon as possible—that is, after he had found out all there was to be found out about his affairs and his habits.

Just a week after the murder, on Saturday evening therefore, the snow was whirling merrily about the gables and cupolas of the Archducal hunting castle. The weather-vanes groaned and the old trees in the park bent their tall tops under the mad wind which swept across the earth and tore the protecting snow covering from their branches. It was a stormy evening, not one to be out in if a man had a warm corner in which to hide.

An old peddler was trying to find shelter from the rapidly increasing storm under the lea of the castle wall. He crouched so close to the stones that he could scarcely be seen at all, in spite of the light from the snow. Finally he disappeared altogether behind one of the heavy columns which sprang out at intervals from the magnificent wall. Only his head peeped out occasionally as if looking for something. His dark, thoughtful eyes glanced over the little village spread out on one side of the castle, and over the railway station, its most imposing building. Then they would turn back again to the entrance gate in the wall near where he stood. It was a heavy iron-barred gate, its handsome ornamentation outlined in snow, and behind it the body of a large dog could be occasionally seen. This dog was an enormous grey Ulmer hound.

The peddler stood for a long time motionless behind the pillar, then he looked at his watch. "It's nearly time," he murmured, and looked over towards the station again, where lights and figures were gathering.

At the same time the noise of an opening door was heard, and steps creaked over the snow. A man, evidently a servant, opened the little door beside the great gate and held it for another man to pass out. "You'll come back by the night train as usual, sir?" he asked respectfully.

"Yes," replied the other, pushing back the dog, which fawned upon him.

"Come back here, Tristan," called the servant, pulling the dog in by his collar, as he closed the door and re-entered the house.

The Councillor took the path to the station. He walked slowly, with bowed head and uneven step. He did not look like a man who was in the mood to join a merry crowd, and yet he was evidently going to his Club. "He wants to show himself; he doesn't want to let people think that he has anything to be afraid of," murmured the peddler, looking after him sharply. Then his eyes suddenly dimmed and a light sigh was heard, with another murmur, "Poor man." The Councillor reached the station and disappeared within its door. The train arrived and departed a few moments later. Kniepp must have really gone to the city, for although the man behind the pillar waited for some little time, the Councillor did not return—a contingency that the peddler had not deemed improbable.

About half an hour after the departure of the train the watcher came out of his hiding place and walked noisily past the gate. What he expected, happened. The dog rushed up to the bars, barking loudly, but when the peddler had taken a silk muffler from the pack on his back and held it out to the animal, the noise ceased and the dog's anger turned to friendliness. Tristan was quite gentle, put his huge head up to the bars to let the stranger pat it, and seemed not at all alarmed when the latter rang the bell.

The young man who had opened the door for the Councillor came out from a wing of the castle. The peddler looked so frozen and yet so venerable that the youth had not the heart to turn him away. Possibly he was glad of a little diversion for his own sake.

"Who do you want to see?" he asked.

"I want to speak to the maid, the one who attended your dead mistress."

"Oh, then you know—?"

"I know of the misfortune that has happened here."

"And you think that Nanette might have something to sell to you?"

"Yes, that's it; that's why I came. For I don't suppose there's much chance for any business with my cigar holders and other trifles here so near the city."

"Cigar holders? Why, I don't know; perhaps we can make a trade. Come in with me. Why, just see how gentle the dog is with you!"

"Isn't he that way with everybody? I supposed he was no watchdog."

"Oh, indeed he is. He usually won't allow anybody to touch him, except those whom he knows well. I'm astonished that he lets you come to the house at all."

They had reached the door by this time. The peddler laid his hand on the servant's arm and halted a moment. "Where was it that she threw herself out?"

"From the last window upstairs there."

"And did it kill her at once?"

"Yes. Anyway she was unconscious when we came down."

"Was the master at home?"

"Why, yes, it happened in the middle of the night."

"She had a fever, didn't she? Had she been ill long?"

"No. She was in bed that day, but we thought it was nothing of importance."

"These fevers come on quickly sometimes," remarked the old man wisely, and added: "This case interests the entire neighbourhood and I will show you that I can be grateful for anything you may tell me— of course, only what a faithful servant could tell. It will interest my customers very much."

"You know all there is to know," said the valet, evidently disappointed that he had nothing to tell which could win the peddler's gratitude. "There are no secrets about it. Everybody knows that they were a very happy couple, and even if there was a little talk between them on that day, why it was pure accident and had nothing to do with the mistress' excitement."

"Then there was a quarrel between them?"

"Are people talking about it?"

"I've heard some things said. They even say that this quarrel was the reason for—her death."

"It's stupid nonsense!" exclaimed the servant. The old peddler seemed to like the young man's honest indignation.

While they were talking, they had passed through a long corridor and the young man laid his hand on one of the doors as the peddler asked, "Can I see Miss Nanette alone?"

"Alone? Oho, she's engaged to me!"

"I know that," said the stranger, who seemed to be initiated into all the doings of this household. "And I am an old man—all I meant was that I would rather not have any of the other servants about."

"I'll keep the cook out of the way if you want me to."

"That would be a good idea. It isn't easy to talk business before others," remarked the old man as they entered the room. It was a comfortably furnished and cozily warm apartment. Only two people were there, an old woman and a pretty young girl, who both looked up in astonishment as the men came in.

"Who's this you're bringing in, George?" asked Nanette.

"He's a peddler and he's got some trifles here you might like to look at."

"Why, yes, you wanted a thimble, didn't you, Lena?" asked Nanette, and the cook beckoned to the peddler. "Let's see what you've got there," she said in a friendly tone. The old man pulled out his wares from his pack; thimbles and scissors, coloured ribbons, silks, brushes and combs, and many other trifles. When the women had made their several selections they noticed that the old man was shivering with the cold, as he leaned against the stove. Their sympathies were aroused in a moment. "Why don't you sit down?" asked Nanette, pushing a chair towards him, and Lena rose to get him something warm from the kitchen.

The peddler threw a look at George, who nodded in answer. "He said he'd like to see the things they gave you after Mrs. Kniepp's death," the young man remarked,

"Do you buy things like that?" Nanette turned to the peddler.

"I'd just like to look at them first, if you'll let me."

"I'd be glad to get rid of them. But I won't go upstairs, I'm afraid there." "Well, I'll get the things for you if you want me to," offered George and turned to leave the room. The door had scarcely closed behind him when a change came over the peddler. His old head rose from its drooping position, his bowed figure started up with youthful elasticity.

"Are you really fond of him?" he asked of the astonished Nanette, who stepped back a pace, stammering in answer: "Yes. Why do you ask? and who are you?"

"Never mind that, my dear child, but just answer the questions I have to ask, and answer truthfully, or it might occur to me to let your George know that he is not the first man you have loved."

"What do you know?" she breathed in alarm.

The peddler laughed. "Oho, then he's jealous! All the better for me—the Councillor was jealous too, wasn't he?" Nanette looked at him in horror.

"The truth, therefore, you must tell me the truth, and get the others away, so I can speak to you alone. You must do this—or else I'll tell George about the handsome carpenter in Church street, or about Franz Schmid, or—"

"For God's sake, stop—stop—I'll do anything you say."

The girl sank back on her chair pale and trembling, while the peddler resumed his pose of a tired old man leaning against the stove. When George returned with a large basket, Nanette had calmed herself sufficiently to go about the unpacking of the articles in the hamper.

"George, won't you please keep Lena out in the kitchen. Ask her to make some tea for us," asked Nanette with well feigned assurance. George smiled a meaning smile and disappeared.

"I am particularly interested in the dead lady's gloves," said the peddler when they were alone again.

Nanette looked at him in surprise but was still too frightened to offer any remarks. She opened several boxes and packages and laid a number of pairs of gloves on the table. The old man looked through them, turning them over carefully. Then he shook his head: "There must be some more somewhere," he said. Nanette was no longer astonished at anything he might say or do, so she obediently went through the basket again and found a little box in which were several pair of grey suede gloves, fastened by bluish mother-of-pearl buttons. One of the pairs had been worn, and a button was missing.

"These are the ones I was looking for," said the peddler, putting the gloves in his pocket. Then he continued: "Your mistress was rather fond of taking long walks by herself, wasn't she?"

The girl's pale face flushed hotly and she stammered: "You know—about it?"

"You know about it also, I see. And did you know everything?"

"Yes, everything," murmured Nanette.

"Then it was you and Tristan who accompanied the lady on her walks?"

"Yes."

"I supposed she must have taken some one into her confidence. Well, and what do you think about the murder?"

"The Professor?" replied Nanette hastily. "Why, what should I know about it?"

"The Councillor was greatly excited and very unhappy when he discovered this affair, I suppose?"

"He is still."

"And how did he act after the—let us call it the accident?"

"He was like a crazy man."

"They tell me that he went about his duties just the same—that he went away on business."

"It wasn't business this time, at least not professional business. But before that he did have to go away frequently for weeks at a time."

"And it was then that your mistress was most interested in her lonely walks, eh?"

"Yes." Nanette's voice was so low as to be scarcely heard.

"Well, and this time?" continued the peddler. "Why did he go away this time?"

"He went to the capital on private business of his own."

"Are you sure of that?"

"Quite sure. He went two different times. I thought it was because he couldn't stand it here and wanted to see something different. He went to his club this evening, too."

"And when did he go away?"

"The first time was the day after his wife was buried."

"And the second time?"

"Two or three days after his return."

"How long did he stay away the first time?"

"Only one day."

"Good! Pull yourself together now. I'll send your George in to you and tell him you haven't been feeling well. Don't tell any one about our conversation. Where is the kitchen?"

"The last door to the right down the hall."

The peddler left the room and Nanette sank down dazed and trembling on the nearest chair. George found her still pale, but he seemed to think it quite natural that she should have been overcome by the recollection of the terrible death of her mistress. He gave the old man a most cordial invitation to return during the next few days. The cook brought the peddler a cup of steaming tea, and purchased several trifles from him, before he left the house.

When the old man had reached a lonely spot on the road, about half way between the hunting castle and the city, he halted, set down his pack, divested himself of his beard and his wig and washed the wrinkles from his face with a handful of snow from the wayside. A quarter of an hour later, Detective Muller entered the railway station of the city, burdened with a large grip. He took a seat in the night express which rolled out from the station a few moments later.

As he was alone in his compartment, Muller gave way to his excitement, sometimes even murmuring half-aloud the thoughts that rushed through his brain. "Yes, I am convinced of it, but can I find the proofs?" the words came again and again, and in spite of the comfortable warmth in the compartment, in spite of his tired and half-frozen condition, he could not sleep.

He reached the capital at midnight and took a room in a small hotel in a quiet street. When he went out next morning, the servants looked after him with suspicion, as in their opinion a man who spent most of the night pacing up and down his room must surely have a guilty conscience.

Muller went to police headquarters and looked through the arrivals at the hotels on the 21st of November. The burial of Mrs. Kniepp had taken place on the 20th. Muller soon found the name he was looking for, "Forest Councillor Leo Kniepp," in the list of guests at the Hotel Imperial. The detective went at once to the Hotel Imperial, where he was already well known. It cost him little time and trouble to discover what he wished to know, the reason for the Councillor's visit to the capital.

Kniepp had asked for the address of a goldsmith, and had been directed to one of the shops which had the best reputation in the city. He had been in the capital altogether for about twenty-four hours. He had the manner and appearance of a man suffering under some terrible blow.

Muller himself was deep in thought as he entered the train to return to his home, after a visit to the goldsmith in question. He had a short interview with Chief of Police Bauer, who finally gave him the golden bullet and the keys to the apartment of the murdered man. Then the two went out together.

An hour later, the chief of police and Muller stood in the garden of the house in which the murder had occurred. Bauer had entered from the Promenade after Muller had shown him how to work the lock of the little gate. Together they went up into the apartment, which was icy cold and uncanny in its loneliness. But the two men did not appear to notice this, so greatly were they interested in the task that had brought them there. First of all, they made a most minute examination of the two doors which had been locked. The keys were still in both locks on the inside. They were big heavy keys, suitable for the tall massive heavily-panelled and iron-ornamented doors. The entire villa was built in this heavy old German style, the favourite fashion of the last few years.

When they had looked the locks over carefully, Muller lit the lamp that hung over the desk in the study and closed the window shutters tight. Bauer had smiled at first as he watched his protege's actions, but his smile changed to a look of keen interest as he suddenly understood. Muller took his place in the chair before the desk and looked over at the door of the vestibule, which was directly opposite him. "Yes, that's all right," he said with a deep breath.

Bauer had sat down on the sofa to watch the proceedings, now he sprang up with an exclamation: "Through the keyhole?"

"Through the keyhole," answered Muller.

"It is scarcely possible."

"Shall we try it?"

"Yes, yes, you do it." Even the usually indifferent old chief of police was breathing more hastily now. Muller took a roll of paper and a small pistol out of his pocket. He unrolled the paper, which represented the figure of a French soldier with a marked target on the breast. The detective pinned the paper on the back of the chair in which Professor Fellner had been seated when he met his death.

"But the key was in the hole," objected Bauer suddenly.

"Yes, but it was turned so that the lower part of the hole was free. Johann saw the light streaming through and could look into the room. If the murderer put the barrel of his pistol to this open part of the keyhole, the bullet would have to strike exactly where the dead man sat. There would be no need to take any particular aim." Muller gazed into space like a seer before whose mental eye a vision has arisen, and continued in level tones: "Fellner had refused the duel and the murderer was crazed by his desire for revenge. He came here to the house, he must have known just how to enter the place, how to reach the rooms, and he must have known also, that the Professor, coward as he was—"

"Coward? Is a man a coward when he refuses to stand up to a maniac?" interrupted Bauer.

Muller came back to the present with a start and said calmly, "Fellner was a coward."

"Then you know more than you are telling me now?"

Muller nodded. "Yes, I do," he answered with a smile. "But I will tell you more only when I have all the proofs in my own hand."

"And the criminal will escape us in the meantime."

"He has no idea that he is suspected."

"But—you'll promise to be sensible this time, Muller?"

"Yes. But you will pardon me my present reticence, even towards you? I—I don't want to be thought a dreamer again."

"As in the Kniepp case?"

"As in the Kniepp case," repeated the little man with a strange smile. "So please allow me to go about it in my own way. I will tell you all you want to know to-morrow."

"To-morrow, then."

"May I now continue to unfold my theories?" Bauer nodded and Muller continued: "The criminal wanted Fellner's blood, no matter how."

"Even if it meant murder," said Bauer.

Muller nodded calmly. "It would have been nobler, perhaps, to have warned his victim of his approach, but it might have all come to nothing then. The other could have called for help, could have barricaded himself in his room, one crime might have been prevented, and another, more shameful one, would have gone unavenged."

"Another crime? Fellner a criminal?"

"To-morrow you shall know everything, my kind friend. And now, let us make the trial. Please lock the door behind me as it was locked then."

Muller left the room, taking the pistol with him. Bauer locked the door. "Is this right?" he asked.

"Yes, I can see a wide curve of the room, taking in the entire desk. Please stand to one side now."

There was deep silence for a moment, then a slight sound as of metal on metal, then a report, and Muller re-entered the study through the bedroom. He found Bauer stooping over the picture of the French soldier. There was a hole in the left breast, where the bullet, passing through, had buried itself in the back of the chair.

"Yes, it was all just as you said," began the chief of police, holding out his hand to Muller. "But—why the golden bullet?"

"To-morrow, to-morrow," replied the detective, looking up at his superior with a glance of pleading.

They left the house together and in less than an hour's time Muller was again in the train rolling towards the capital.

He went to the goldsmith's shop as soon as he arrived. The proprietor received him with eager interest and Muller handed him the golden bullet. "Here is the golden object of which I spoke," said the detective, paying no heed to the other's astonishment. The goldsmith opened a small locked drawer, took a ring from it and set about an examination of the two little objects. When he turned to his visitor again, he was evidently satisfied with what he had discovered. "These two objects are made of exactly the same sort of gold, of a peculiar old

French composition, which can no longer be produced in the same richness. The weight of the gold in the bullet is exactly the same as in the ring."

"Would you be willing to take an oath on that if you were called in as an expert?"

"I am willing to stand up for my judgment."

"Good. And now will you read this over please, it contains the substance of what you told me yesterday. Should I have made any mistakes, please correct them, for I will ask you to set your signature to it."

Muller handed several sheets of close writing to the goldsmith and the latter read aloud as follows: "On the 22nd of November, a gentleman came into my shop and handed me a wedding ring with the request that I should make another one exactly like it. He was particularly anxious that the work should be done in two days at the very latest, and also that the new ring, in form, colour, and in the engraving on the inside, should be a perfect counterpart of the first. He explained his order by saying that his wife was ill, and that she was grieving over the loss of her wedding ring which had somehow disappeared. The new ring could be found somewhere as if by chance and the sick woman's anxiety would be over. Two days later, as arranged, the same gentleman appeared again and I handed him the two rings.

"He left the shop, greatly satisfied with my work and apparently much relieved in his mind. But he left me uneasy in spirit because I had deceived him. It had not been possible for me to reproduce exactly the composition of the original ring, and as I believed that the work was to be done in order to comfort an invalid, and I was getting no profit, but on the contrary a little extra work out of it, I made two new rings, lettered them according to the original and gave them to my customer. The original ring I am now, on this seventh day of December, giving to Mr. Joseph Mullet, who has shown me his legitimation as a member of the Secret Police. I am willing to put myself at the service of the authorities if I am called for."

"You are willing to do this, aren't you?" asked Muller when the goldsmith had arrived at the end of the notice.

"Of course."

"Have you anything to add to this?"

"No, it is quite complete. I will sign it at once."

Several hours later, Muller re-entered the police station in his home town and saw the windows of the chief's apartment brilliantly lighted. "What's going on," he asked of Bauer's servant who was just hurrying up the stairs.

"The mistress' birthday, we've got company."

Muller grumbled something and went on up to his own room. He knew it would not be pleasant for his patron to be disturbed in the midst of entertaining his guests, but the matter was important and could not wait.

The detective laid off his outer garments, made a few changes in his toilet and putting the goldsmith's declaration, with the ring and the bullet in his pocketbook, he went down to the first floor of the building, in one wing of which was the apartment occupied by the Chief. He sent in his name and was told to wait in the little study. He sat down quietly in a corner of the comfortable little room beyond which, in a handsomely furnished smoking room, a number of guests sat playing cards. From the drawing rooms beyond, there was the sound of music and many voices.

It was all very attractive and comfortable, and the solitary man sat there enjoying once more the pleasant sensation of triumph, of joy at the victory that was his alone and that would win him back all his old friends and prestige. He was looking forward in agreeable anticipation to the explanations he had to give, when he suddenly started and grew pale. His eyes dimmed a moment, then he pulled himself together and murmured: "No, no, not this time. I will not be weak this time."

Just then the Chief entered the room, accompanied by Councillor Kniepp.

"Won't you sit down here a little?" asked the friendly host. "You will find it much quieter in this room." He pulled up a little table laden with cigars and wine, close to a comfortable armchair. Then, noticing Muller, he continued with a friendly nod: "I'm glad they told you to wait in here. You must be frozen after your long ride. If you will wait just a moment more, I will return at once and we can go into my office. And if you will make yourself comfortable here, my dear Kniepp, I will send our friend Horn in to talk with you. He is bright and jovial and will keep you amused."

The chief chattered on, making a strenuous endeavour to appear quite harmless. But Kniepp, more apt than ever just now to notice the actions of others, saw plainly that his genial host was concealing some excitement. When the latter had gone out the Councillor looked after him, shaking his head. Then his glance fell by chance on the quiet-looking man who had risen at his entrance and had not sat down again.

"Please sit down," he said in a friendly tone, but the other did not move. His grey eyes gazed intently at the man whose fate he was to change so horribly.

Kniepp grew uneasy under the stare. "What is there that interests you so about me?" he asked in a tone that was an attempt at a joke.

"The ring, the ring on your watch chain," murmured Muller.

"It belonged to my dead wife. I have worn it since she left me," answered the unhappy man with the same iron calm with which he had, all these past days, been emphasizing his love for the woman he had lost. Yet the question touched him unpleasantly and he looked more sharply at the strange man over in the corner. He saw the latter's face turn pale and a shiver run through his form. A feeling of sympathy came over Kniepp and he asked warmly: "Won't you take a glass of this wine? If you have been out in the cold it will be good for you." His tone was gentle, almost cordial, but the man to whom he offered the refreshment turned from him with a gesture that was almost one of terror.

The Councillor rose suddenly from his chair. "Who are you? What news is it you bring?" he asked with a voice that began to tremble.

Muller raised his head sharply as if his decision had been made, and his kind intelligent eyes grew soft as they rested on the pale face of the stately man before him. "I belong to the Secret Police and I am compelled to find out the secrets of others—not because of my profession—no, because my own nature compels me—I must do it. I have just come from Vienna and I bring the last of the proofs necessary to turn you over to the courts. And yet you are a thousand times better than the coward who stole the honour of your wife and who hid behind the shelter of the law—and therefore, therefore, therefore—" Muller's voice grew hoarse, then died away altogether.

Kniepp listened with pallid cheeks but without a quiver. Now he spoke, completing the other's words: "And therefore you wish to save me from the prison or from the gallows? I thank you. What is your name?" The unhappy man spoke as calmly as if the matter scarcely concerned him at all.

The detective told him his name.

"Muller, Muller," repeated the Councillor, as if he were particularly anxious to remember the name. He held out his hand to the detective. "I thank you, indeed, thank you," he said with the first sign of emotion he had shown, and then added low: "Do not fear that you will have trouble on my account. They can find me in my home." With these words he turned away and sat down in his chair again. When Bauer entered the room a few moments later, Kniepp was smoking calmly.

"Now, Muller, I'm ready. Horn will be in in a moment, friend Kniepp; I know you will enjoy his chatter." The chief led the way out of the room through another door. He could not see the ghastly pale face of the guest he left behind him, for it was almost hidden in a cloud of thick smoke, but Muller turned back once more at the threshold and caught a last grateful glance from eyes shadowed by deep sadness, as the Councillor raised his hand in a friendly gesture.

"Dear Muller, you take so long to get at the point of the story! Don't you see you are torturing me?" This outburst came from the Chief about an hour later. But the detective would not permit himself to be interrupted in spinning out his story in his own way, and it was nearly another hour before Bauer knew that the man for whose name he had been waiting so long was Leo Kniepp.

The knowledge came as a terrible surprise to him. He was dazed almost. "And I,—I've got to arrest him in my own house?" he exclaimed as if horrified. And Muller answered calmly: "I doubt if you will have the opportunity, sir."

"Muller! Did you, again—"

"Yes, I did! I have again warned an unfortunate. It's my nature, I can't seem to help it. But you will find the Councillor in his house. He promised me that."

"And you believe it?"

"That man will keep his promise," said Muller quietly.

Councillor Kniepp did keep his promise. When the police arrived at the hunting castle shortly after midnight, they found the terrified servants standing by the body of their master.

"Well, Muller, you had better luck than you deserved this time," Bauer said a few days later. "This last trick has made you quite impossible for the service. But you needn't worry about that, because the legacy Kniepp left you will put you out of reach of want."

The detective was as much surprised as anybody. He was as if dazed by his unexpected good fortune. The day before he was a poor man bowed under the weight of sordid cares, and now he was the possessor of twenty thousand gulden. And it was not his clever brain but his warm heart that had won this fortune for him. His breast swelled with gratitude as he thought of the unhappy man whose life had been ruined by the careless cruelty of others and his own passions. Again and again he read the letter which had been found on Kniepp's desk, addressed to him and which had been handed out to him after the inquest.

My friend: —
You have saved me from the shame of an open trial. I thank you
for this from the very depth of my heart. I have left you a
part of my own private fortune, that you may be a free man, free
as a poor man never can be. You can accept this present for it
comes from the hand of an honest man in spite of all. Yes, I
compelled my wife to go to her death after I had compelled her
to confess her shame to me, and I entered her lover's house with
the knowledge I had forced from her. When I looked through the
keyhole and saw his false face before me, I murdered him in cold
blood. Then, that the truth might not be suspected, I continued
to play the sorrowing husband. I wore on my watch chain the ring
I had had made in imitation of the one my wife had worn. This
original ring of hers, her wedding ring which she had defiled,
I sent in the form of a bullet straight to her lover's heart.
Yes, I have committed a crime, but I feel that I am less criminal
than those two whom I judged and condemned, and whose sentence I
carried out as I now shall carry out my own sentence with a hand
which will not tremble. That I can do this myself, I have you to
thank for, you who can look into the souls of men and recognise
the most hidden motives, you who have not only a wonderful brain

but a heart that can feel. You, I hope, will sometimes think
kindly of your grateful
LEO KNIEPP.

Muller kept this letter as one of his most sacred treasures.

The "Kniepp Case" was really, as Bauer had predicted, the last in Muller's public career. Even the friendliness of the kind old chief could not keep him in his position after this new display of the unreliability of his heart. But his quiet tastes allowed him to live in humble comfort from the income of his little fortune.

Every now and then letters or telegrams will come for him and he will disappear for several days. His few friends believe that the police authorities, who refused to employ him publicly owing to his strange weakness, cannot resist a private appeal to his talent whenever a particularly difficult case arises.